More **Dark Man** books:

First series

The Dark Fire of Doom
Destiny in the Dark
The Dark Never Hides

D0121034

The Face in the Dark Mirror	978-184167-411-7
Fear in the Dark	978-184167-412-4
Escape from the Dark	978-184167-416-2
Danger in the Dark	978-184167-415-5
The Dark Dreams of Hell	978-184167-418-6
The Dark Side of Magic	978-184167-414-8
The Dark Glass	978-184167-421-6
The Dark Waters of Time	978-184167-413-1
The Shadow in the Dark	978-184167-420-9

Second series

The Dark Candle	978-184167-603-6
The Dark Machine	978-184167-601-2
The Dark Words	978-184167-602-9
Dying for the Dark	978-184167-604-3
Kil	'-605-0
Th	'-606-7

Dark Man

The Dark Fire of Doom
by Peter Lancett
illustrated by Jan Pedroietta

Published by Ransom Publishing Ltd.
Radley House, 8 St. Cross Road, Winchester, Hampshire
SO23 9HX
www.ransom.co.uk

ISBN 978 184167 417 9

First published in 2005
Reprinted 2007, 2009, 2011

Dark Man

The Dark Fire
of Doom

by Peter Lancett

illustrated by Jan Pedroietta

Rans**m

Chapter One:
The Tunnels

Secret tunnels run under the bad part of the city.

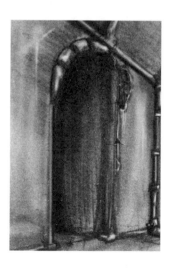

All the tunnels have a nasty smell.

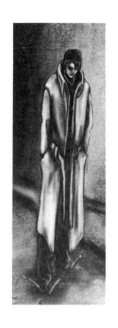

The Dark Man does not care.

He has been in the tunnels many times.

The Dark Man cannot see in the tunnel.

There is no light.

He steps with great care.

The Dark Man looks for a magic flame.

The Old Man said it was down here.

Chapter Two:
The Boy

The Dark Man hears a secret word.

He stops.

A boy stands in front of him.

"I can take you to the fire," the boy says.

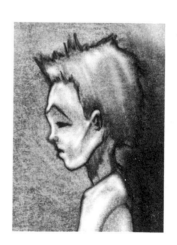

The Dark Man follows the boy.

He cannot see where they are going.

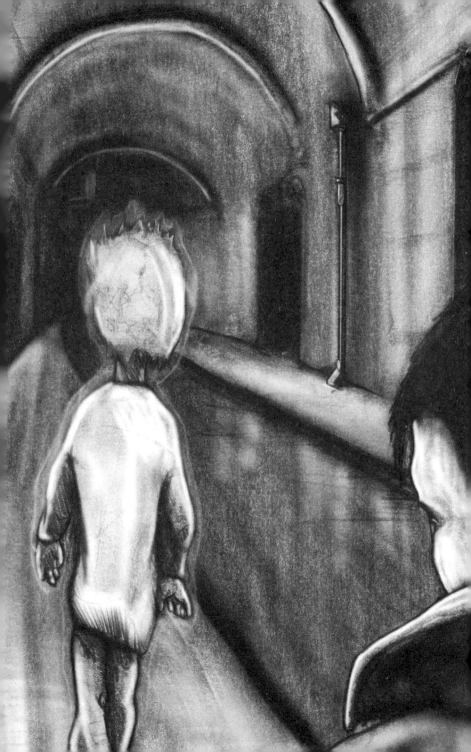

After a long walk, the boy stops.

"It is around the corner," he says.

Chapter Three:
The Fire

The Dark Man steps into the new tunnel
alone.

A flame burns in the side of the wall.

This fire is an evil gateway used by demons.

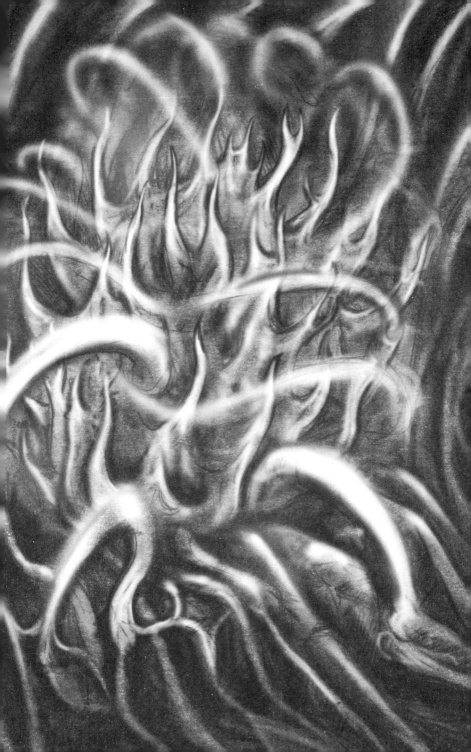

The Dark Man knows what he must do.

He puts his hand into the flame.

He has no fear so the fire does not burn him.

There is a great flash.

Chapter Four:
It is Done

When the Dark Man opens his eyes, he is lying on cool grass.

His hand is not burnt.

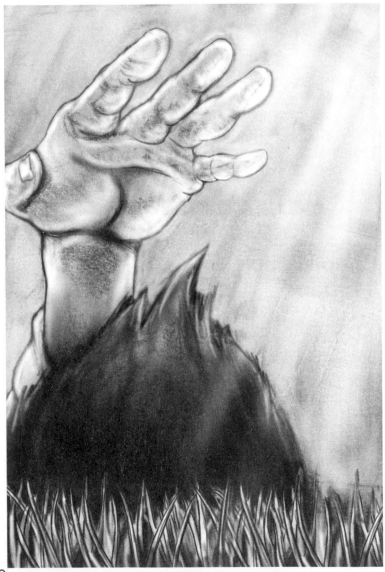